This Book Belongs to

_____

A FABER PICTURE BOOK

The Goat

Café

Francesca Simon

Illustrated by Leo Broadley

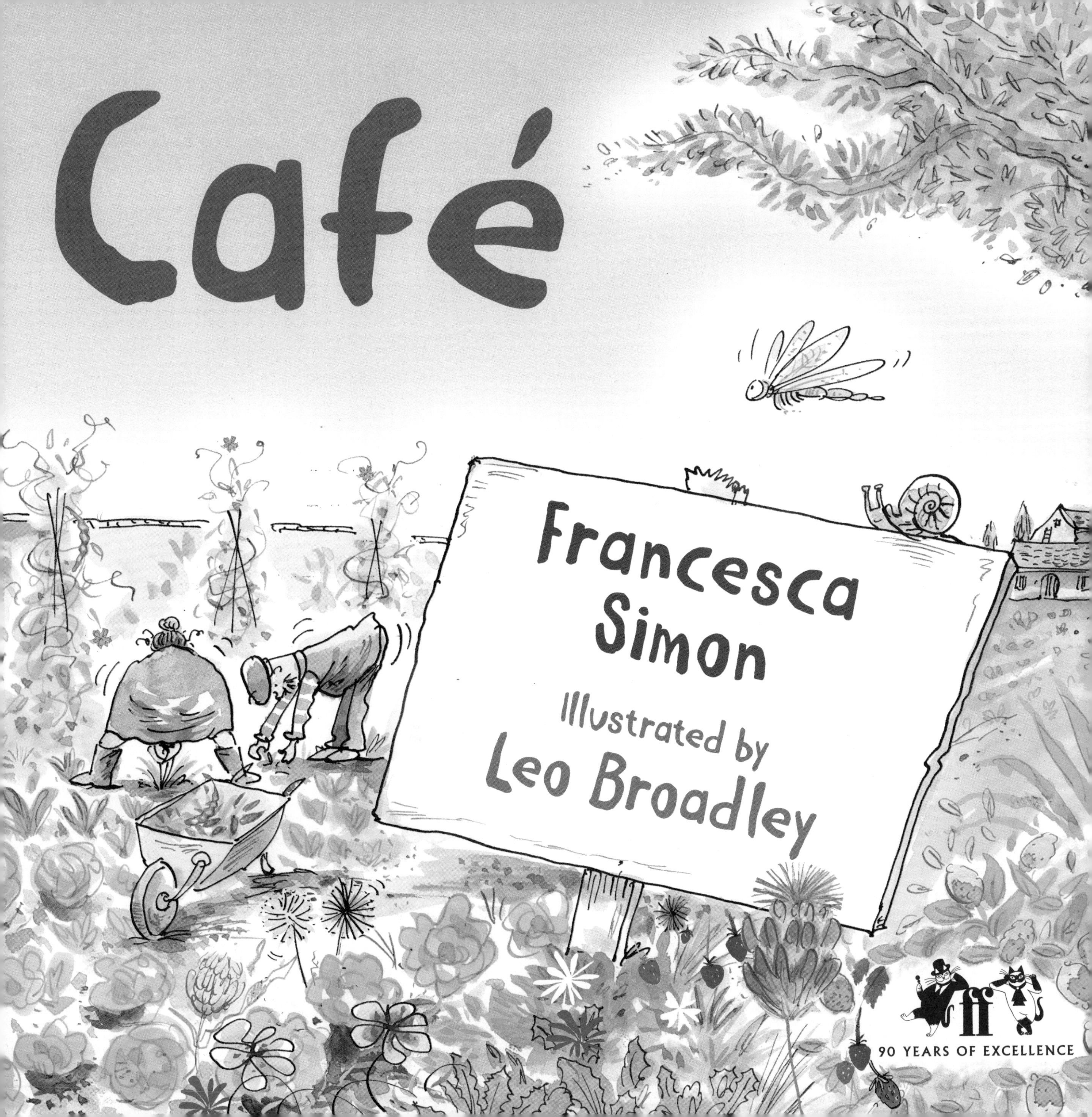

ff 90 YEARS OF EXCELLENCE

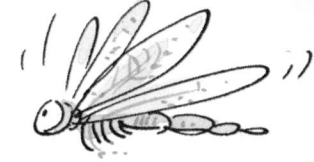

It's Monday.
Look, kids, look!
The new Goat Café.

Hurray!

What's on the menu for today?

Strawberries
OOH

Artichokes
CHEW

Beans
So beany

And yum!
Bamboo!

MUNCH

CRUNCH
CRUNCH

And for dessert they ate the U and the T.

MAAAAAAAAAAAAAAAAAAAH
said the goats MAAAAAAAAAAAAAAAA

It's Tuesday.

Hurray!

What's on the menu
at The Goat Café?

And for dessert they ate the O.

MAAAAAAAAAAAAAAAAAAAAAAH
said the goats

MAAAAAAAAAAAAAAAAAA

And for dessert they ate the P, E and E.

MAAAAAAAAAAAAAAAAAAAH
said the goats

MAAAAAAAAAAAAAA

NO GOATS!
K

It's Thursday. **Hurray!** What's on the menu at The Goat Café?

Grass
DELIGHTFUL!

Honeysuckle DIVINE!
Brambles fresh from the ground

What a treat.

And the ivy—
So spicy! So juicy!
So sweet.

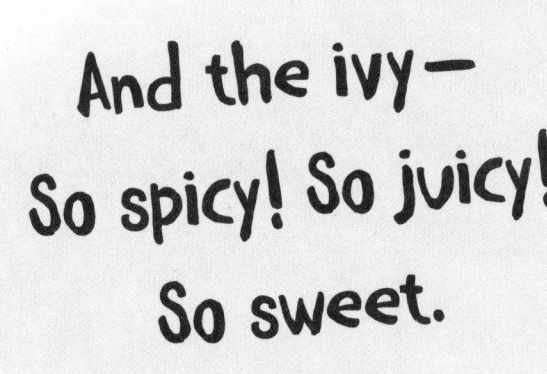

MUNCH
CRUNCH
CRUNCH

And for dessert they ate the K

MAAAAAAAAAAAAAAAAH
said the goats
MAAAAAAAAAAAAAAA

NO GOATS!

It's Friday. **Hurray!**
What's on the menu
                    at The Goat Café?

And for dessert
they ate the N.

MAAAAAAAAAAAAAAAAAAH
said the goats

MAAAAAAAAAAAAAAAA

It's Sunday.

Booooooo!

There's nothing on the menu
at The Goat Café.

But
wait . . .

MAAAAAAAAAA

For Ava and Jesse, who first dined at The Goat Café
F. S.

To Katie, Megan, Roisin, Evelinn and Henry
Cheers, Leo

First published in the UK in 2019. First published in the USA in 2019 by Faber and Faber Limited
Bloomsbury House, 74–77 Great Russell Street, London WC1B 3DA and Profile Books, 3 Holford yard, Bevin way, London WC1X 9HO
www.profilebooks.com

HB ISBN 978-0-571-32867-3
PB ISBN 978-0-571-32869-7

Printed in India

10 9 8 7 6 5 4 3 2 1

FABER & FABER has published children's books since 1929. Some of our very first publications included *Old Possum's Book of Practical Cats* by T. S. Eliot starring the now world-famous Macavity, and *The Iron Man* by Ted Hughes. Our catalogue at the time said that 'it is by reading such books that children learn the difference between the shoddy and the genuine'. We still believe in the power of reading to transform children's lives.